Dead Ringer

by Gino DiIorio

A SAMUEL FRENCH ACTING EDITION

SAMUEL FRENCH

FOUNDED 1830

NEW YORK HOLLYWOOD LONDON TORONTO

SAMUELFRENCH.COM

MUSIC USE NOTE

Licensees are solely responsible for obtaining formal written permission from copyright owners to use copyrighted music in the performance of this play and are strongly cautioned to do so. If no such permission is obtained by the licensee, then the licensee must use only original music that the licensee owns and controls. Licensees are solely responsible and liable for all music clearances and shall indemnify the copyright owners of the play and their licensing agent, Samuel French, Inc., against any costs, expenses, losses and liabilities arising from the use of music by licensees.

IMPORTANT BILLING AND CREDIT REQUIREMENTS

All producers of *DEAD RINGER must* give credit to the Author of the Play in all programs distributed in connection with performances of the Play, and in all instances in which the title of the Play appears for the purposes of advertising, publicizing or otherwise exploiting the Play and/or a production. The name of the Author *must* appear on a separate line on which no other name appears, immediately following the title and *must* appear in size of type not less than fifty percent of the size of the title type.

DEAD RINGER was first produced by the New Jersey Repertory Company in Long Branch, New Jersey on October 15, 2009. The performance was directed by Suzanne Barabas, with sets by Jessica Parks, costumes by Patricia E. Doherty, lighting by Jill Nagle, and sound by Merek Royca Press. The production stage manager was Rose Riccardi. The cast was as follows:

DWIGHT . . . . Christian Pedersen

TYRUS . . . . Michael Pollard

MARY . . . . Natalie Wilder

CHARACTERS

DWIGHT FOLEY – 30. A heavyset man with a thin beard. He has an inno-
cence about him that borders on naiveté. He is not confident and
can easily be hurt with harsh words.

MARY COLE – 28. The woman in the hole. She is never seen throughout
the course of the play. She has many physical ailments and deformi-
ties. Her head is misshapen and she cannot walk. But she manages
to feed and clean herself as the strength of her arms allows her
to move about her small space. Mary is very intelligent, carrying
herself with a hard edge of sarcasm and wit. She has a voice like
an angel and at times, displays a mystical quality. Mary has no self-
pity whatsoever and one gets the impression that had it not been
for her physical defects, she could easily win a fist fight with her
brother.

TYRUS COLE – 35. Mary's older brother. He is tall and muscular, clean
shaven with hard, angular features. Ty wears the burden of his sister's ailment on his sleeve. His cruelty toward her is born more of
self-loathing than sadism.

SETTING

Sunset Valley, Texas

TIME

Spring, 1880

AUTHOR'S NOTES

The set should not be a realistic representation of the Cole farm. Rather,
the space should have an "otherworldly" feel to it. The acting style
should be reserved as well. For lack of a better term, these characters
are much closer to the film *Unforgiven* than, say, the television drama
Bonanza.

Scene One

(Lights up on the farm of **TYRUS COLE**. *There is a desolate farm house with a porch stage left and a large barn heading back a ways, with horse stalls and such. Adjacent to the house there is what looks like a root cellar. It has a cage door with slots in it that is heavily padlocked.)*

*(***DWIGHT FOLEY** *walks toward the porch. He is heavyset with a thin beard. His clothes are dusty and he has mud on his face. His blue denim shirt is practically soaked through.)*

DWIGHT. Hey Ty. Ty Cole, you in there?

*(***DWIGHT** *walks up on the porch and peeks in through the window)*

It's me Dwight. Ty? Hello?

(He looks up at the sky and considers whether or not he should wait. He jumps down off the porch and looks out around the house and then speaks quietly.)

Aw shoot. Where the hell are ya?

(We hear **MARY** *call from the root cellar. She is not seen throughout the play.)*

MARY. *(offstage)* Stay right where you are.

DWIGHT. Who's that?

MARY. I said stay where you are or I'll blast your head off.

DWIGHT. Who?

MARY. Stay still!

DWIGHT. Sorry.

MARY. Don't think I won't shoot you cause I will.

DWIGHT. Where the hell?

7

MARY. Move over where I can see you.

(He moves back toward where he entered.)

The other way, you numb skull.

DWIGHT. I don't know where you are.

MARY. I'm down here.

DWIGHT. Where?

MARY. Here.

*(**DWIGHT** approaches the root cellar.)*

Don't move. You looking for Ty?

DWIGHT. Yeah, who are you?

MARY. I'm his sister.

DWIGHT. I didn't know he had no sister.

MARY. Well, he does.

DWIGHT. Is he gonna be back?

MARY. Probably by nightfall. What you want?

DWIGHT. I got a mare and I'm having trouble with it. Thought he might give me some advice.

MARY. Not for free he won't.

DWIGHT. I could pay him.

MARY. Really? How much you got?

DWIGHT. Three dollars and some silver.

MARY. Well, why don't you just put it on the wall of the post office?

DWIGHT. You asked me.

MARY. Don't mean you gotta tell me.

DWIGHT. Well –

MARY. And what are you doing showing up here unannounced?

DWIGHT. What do you mean, unannounced?

MARY. Jesus Christ, do you need map to get dressed in the morning? Unannounced. As in uninvited.

DWIGHT. Oh, I wasn't uninvited. Ty invited me here.

MARY. He did, did he?

DWIGHT. Yeah. He said if I ever needed any help taming a horse, that I should come see him. Shoot everybody knows that. Ty's the best horse trainer around.

MARY. He'd like to think so.

DWIGHT. Well, I could sure use his help.

MARY. He ain't here.

DWIGHT. I know, I can see that.

MARY. He went in to town for some feed. He should be back soon.

DWIGHT. Oh. You mind if I wait?

MARY. Suit yourself. Don't think I'm lowering this gun anytime soon.

DWIGHT. I ain't here to hurt you, I just –

MARY. How the hell do I know that?

DWIGHT. I guess you don't.

MARY. You're right. I don't.

(*pause*)

If you're gonna wait, you may as well sit down.

DWIGHT. On the ground?

MARY. No, I was thinking you might build yourself a table and chairs. Yes, on the ground.

(*He does so. There is a pause.*)

DWIGHT. Awful hot out here.

MARY. I wouldn't know.

DWIGHT. You know, I could just come back later.

MARY. You already came all this way. I'd hate to see you make two trips.

DWIGHT. It's no trouble. I could just mosey on back –

(*He stands.*)

MARY. Sit down.

DWIGHT. Huh?

MARY. Sit back down.

DWIGHT. Okay. (*He sits.*)

MARY. We're gonna sit here and wait till Tyrus comes back and finds out if he knows anybody by the name of... What did you say your name was again?

DWIGHT. Dwight. Dwight Foley. My friends call me Dewey.

MARY. Dewey.

DWIGHT. That's right. And ma'am, Tyrus doesn't –

MARY. Don't call me ma'am, I'm not your mother.

DWIGHT. I'm sorry, I was just being polite.

MARY. You were just being stupid. My name's Mary.

DWIGHT. Oh. Hi Mary.

MARY. Hello.

DWIGHT. Uh, your brother doesn't really know me, see? He just, well, I know of him, you could say. He's the best horse trainer in all – (these parts).

MARY. *(overlapping)* – these parts. You said that already. What if I was to tell you my brother doesn't know a horse's ass from his own pecker? What would you say to that?

DWIGHT. Well, I –

MARY. And maybe you just decided to come up here to rob us, take our stallions or something.

DWIGHT. Come on –

MARY. Or maybe somebody told you that there's a great deal of money somewhere's on this property and you come up here to go fishing for it.

DWIGHT. I don't know what you're talking about.

MARY. The hell you don't.

DWIGHT. Even if I did...

MARY. Yeah?

DWIGHT. Well, I wouldn't do that.

MARY. I guess we're gonna find out, ain't we.

　　(pause)

DWIGHT. Just came up here for some help.

MARY. You'll get your help. In good time.

DWIGHT. Can I ask you a question?

MARY. You just did.

DWIGHT. What?

MARY. Ask a question.

DWIGHT. Oh. Well can I?

MARY. You did it again. You wanna ask another?

DWIGHT. Can I ask another question?

MARY. Did they bring you up on the stupid farm? You did it again!

DWIGHT. Well what am I supposed to say?

MARY. You gotta say, "Can I ask TWO questions?"

DWIGHT. Oh. Can I ask two questions?

MARY. No.

DWIGHT. Damn it –

MARY. All right. Yes, you may ask two questions.

DWIGHT. What are you doing down there?

MARY. None of your business.

DWIGHT. Sorry.

MARY. *(pause)* What's your horse's name?

DWIGHT. Queenie.

MARY. *(She laughs.)* Queenie?

DWIGHT. Yeah.

MARY. What's the matter with Queenie.

DWIGHT. Can't break her.

MARY. No wonder why, you give her a dopey ass name like that.

DWIGHT. Queenie is a good name. I had a dog named Queenie.

MARY. What happened to the dog?

DWIGHT. Died.

MARY. Name probably killed her.

DWIGHT. Shut up.

MARY. What color is Queenie?

DWIGHT. Oh, she's a pretty horse. Kind of a strawberry roan.

MARY. You got yourself a pink horse?

DWIGHT. Well, not exactly –

MARY. She's a red horse with white hair, am I right?

DWIGHT. Yeah, but –

MARY. So what do you get when you mix red with white? You get pink! You got yourself a pink horse!

DWIGHT. I was told she was strawberry roan –

MARY. That's just a polite way of saying pink. You gonna breed her?

DWIGHT. That's the plan, but we had two stallions in with her, but they both ran off.

MARY. Course they did. Who wants to screw a pink horse?

DWIGHT. You stop that now. She scared them off, is what she did.

MARY. Whatever you say.

DWIGHT. See I figured if I can tame her a bit, it might slow her down.

MARY. What's the horse wanna do?

DWIGHT. Run. Won't stay in the stall, just wants to run all the time.

MARY. So let her run.

DWIGHT. I can't let her run. I gotta break her.

MARY. Can you put a saddle on her?

DWIGHT. Hell no. She bucks like crazy.

MARY. How fast is that horse you got there?

DWIGHT. Who, Star? Oh, he's pretty fast.

MARY. Queenie and Star. You sure know how to pick names.

DWIGHT. Forget it. I ain't talking to you.

MARY. All that mare wants to do is run, right?

DWIGHT. I guess.

MARY. So, give her enough rope. Tie one end to the mare and the other to Star. Get on Star and let her run.

DWIGHT. Come on, I'll lose her for sure.

MARY. Maybe you're supposed to lose her.

DWIGHT. What the hell is that supposed to mean?

MARY. Horse is like anything else. You're trying to take part of her spirit away. She don't want to give it to you. You gotta earn her respect.

*(There is a pause as **DWIGHT** considers this.)*

DWIGHT. What's the lock for?

*(There is a sudden gunshot offstage. **DWIGHT** jumps as **TY COLE** enters stage right.)*

TY. What you doing?

DWIGHT. Hello Mr. Cole.

TY. Who told you to come up here?

DWIGHT. I heard you knew about taming horses –

TY. Ain't nobody told you to come up here.

DWIGHT. I'm sorry, I –

TY. What the hell you doing talking to her?

DWIGHT. We was just talking.

*(**DWIGHT** moves away from **TY** and toward the cage.)*

TY. Well, who said you could?

DWIGHT. Nobody, I just come by –

TY. Get the hell away from her.

DWIGHT. Yes sir.

*(**DWIGHT** moves away.)*

MARY. He wasn't doing nothing.

TY. Shut up, you.

*(to **DWIGHT**)*

What's your business here?

DWIGHT. Well uh, Ty – Mr. Cole, I saw you a town a few weeks back and you mentioned to me, or I had heard you mention, you were talking to someone else and I over heard – perhaps I shouldn't have been listening, but I heard you say that, uh…well anyway, I got me a mare I can't tame.

MARY. Name's Queenie.

TY. Would you shut up?!

> (**TY** *walks up to the cage and kicks the bars. He then kicks sand in through the space, down into the cage where* **MARY** *sits.*)

Ain't nobody talking to you.

> (*to* **DWIGHT**)

What's the mare's name?

DWIGHT. Queenie.

TY. (*pause*) What kind of a fool ass name is that?

DWIGHT. Oh hell, I don't know. That's her name, all right? Now you gonna help me tame her?

TY. Sure. Cost you five dollars.

DWIGHT. Aw, come on, I ain't got no five dollars.

TY. Yeah, and you got a horse you can't use.

DWIGHT. Jesus.

> (*He digs through his pockets.*)

I only got but three.

TY. Any silver?

DWIGHT. Uh… (*He digs a bit more.*) …two bits.

TY. Three'll have to do. Two bits will go toward the shells.

> (**DWIGHT** *hesitates, but then hands over the money.*)

Thank you.

> (**TY** *reaches in his pocket and pulls out a shell casing.*)

Let me see your gun.

DWIGHT. I don't have one.

TY. You don't have a gun.

DWIGHT. No sir.

TY. How the hell do you expect to tame that mare without a gun?

DWIGHT. I don't know, Mr. Cole. That's why I came to see you.

MARY. Why don't you just loan him one of yours?

TY. Shut up.

(*pause*)

Tell you what, I'll loan you one of mine.

DWIGHT. Thank you. That's nice of you.

TY. I need something for collateral.

DWIGHT. Collateral. Okay.

TY. What do you got for collateral?

DWIGHT. I don't think I got much of anything.

MARY. Aw, he's good for it.

TY. Will you shut up? Let me see that hat.

DWIGHT. Sure. (*He takes it off.*) It's almost brand new. I got it this winter.

TY. It'll have to do. Gun's worth a lot more.

DWIGHT. Oh, I know that. Don't you worry. I'll bring it right back.

(**TY** *takes his gun out and empties it of shells. He begins putting new shells in.*)

TY. Okay, I'll give you six bullets. You probably won't need more than two, but just in case.

DWIGHT. What do I do?

TY. You go home, you go in that stall and you look her right in the eye and say "Queenie, you dumbass horse, you gonna behave." And you keep saying it till that horse starts to act up. And once it does, you take out that revolver and you fire a shot right above her head. Then you smack her right on the muzzle and say something like, "I give the orders around here," or, "What you mean acting like that." And if she rears up again, you fire another shot. Then you take a saddle and throw it over her back. If she rears, you fire another shot. She probably be scared shitless by then, but that oughta solve the problem.

DWIGHT. Oh. Yeah, all right. That makes sense.

TY. Here. (*He hands* **DWIGHT** *the gun.*) You ever used one of these before?

DWIGHT. Oh sure. This is very nice. Very nice gun.

TY. Uh. Bring back the gun and the bullets you don't use and you get your hat.

DWIGHT. Yessir.

TY. Be careful with that thing.

DWIGHT. I will.

TY. Don't go shooting the damned horse now.

DWIGHT. I won't.

TY. And don't make me come looking for you. I want that gun back by sundown.

DWIGHT. Oh don't worry, I'll be here. Thank you very much.

TY. Good, you get on outta here and give that a try.

DWIGHT. Yessir. Thank you.

TY. Sundown, I want to see you riding that there Queenie. You hear?

DWIGHT. Okay.

(As **DWIGHT** *exits,* **MARY** *calls after him.)*

MARY. Hey Dwight. If that don't work, don't forget what I told you.

*(***TY** *watches him leave.)*

DWIGHT. Oh I will. Good talking to you Mary. *(He exits.)*

TY. What'd I tell you about talking to strangers?

MARY. He was looking for you.

TY. How the hell you know what he wants? What if he ripped that gate open and went down there and had his way with you. How would that be then?

MARY. Who'd wanna do that?

TY. Lotsa folks, believe you me. And what'd you go telling him, anyway?

MARY. I told him how to tame the horse.

TY. Oh yeah? And what technique do you employ?

MARY. Nothing you'd understand.

TY. You got that right.

MARY. Where you been?

TY. In town.

MARY. I'm hungry.

TY. You finish your breakfast?

MARY. This morning.

TY. Well. Let me get settled, I'll fry you up some bacon or something.

MARY. Thank you. Can you empty my pot, too?

TY. I will.

MARY. And I could use some water. I ain't washed –

TY. All right, I heard ya. Damn it, can't you give me a minute for you start making lists of what needs to be done –

MARY. Well, what the hell do you want from me?

TY. *(overlapping)* Yeah, Yeah. I know. All day, all night, sitting there alone –

MARY. *(overlapping)* You got me cooped up here all by myself all day long, if you let you roam about the place –

TY. Roam about the place? And how do you expect to do that?

MARY. I get around just fine.

TY. Yeah, and I come back here and you probably have the whole place lit on fire. No thank you very much.

MARY. Well, you took your sweet time about it.

TY. I had business to attend to. If I don't work, then neither one of us eat, now do we? Do we?

MARY. No.

TY. That's right. No.

MARY. What took you so long?

TY. I ran into that mudsill Donelly, he was having some kinda trouble with a filly that had sand colic. He come by all roostered, "Ty, you gotta help me out."

MARY. Why do you bother with him?

TY. He pays cash money. He'd better. Horse damn near killed us, rolling around, trying to loosen herself up. We ended up walking her for better part of an hour fore she cut loose.

(pause)

What do you think of this piker?

MARY. I don't know. He paid you.

TY. Never see him again. Probably shoot hisself trying to tame that mare.

(TY rises and goes into the house.)

MARY. Where you going?

TY. I thought I might take a nap, if that's all right with you.

MARY. You mind feeding me first?

TY. Let me catch forty winks and then I'll feed us both. Okay?

MARY. Sure.

(TY goes onto the porch, enters the house and closes the door behind him.)

Whatever you say.

(blackout)

Scene Two

*(Early evening. **DWIGHT** moves slowly up toward the house. He looks around tentatively. After a moment, **MARY** calls out to him from the root cellar.)*

MARY. Who's there?

DWIGHT. It's me.

MARY. Who is it?

DWIGHT. It's me, Dwight.

MARY. What do you want?

DWIGHT. I came back to return the gun. And the shells, the ones I didn't use.

MARY. Oh.

DWIGHT. Is Ty at home?

MARY. He's sleeping.

DWIGHT. Oh. Can I leave them with you?

MARY. I don't have your hat.

DWIGHT. Well, I guess maybe he can just give it back when he sees me.

MARY. You best wait till you see him yourself.

DWIGHT. I'm sorry. I didn't know he'd be sleeping. Where's your gun?

MARY. I got it right here. Don't you worry.

DWIGHT. Okay. Well. I'll just come back tomorrow.

MARY. How did it work?

DWIGHT. Oh Good. Worked real good.

MARY. Yeah?

DWIGHT. Sure. I did just like he said. Took that gun and fired it once past her ear and just smacked her on the muzzle. And so she reared up and I said, "Queenie, you're gonna do what I say!" And I fired two more shots. One past her right ear and the other past her left. Pow Pow. Just like that.

MARY. And that did it.

DWIGHT. Sure did. I saddled her and everything.

MARY. You ride her?

DWIGHT. No, not yet. But I'll give her a go tomorrow morning.

MARY. Well. Now you got yourself a horse.

DWIGHT. Yeah. Sure do. Can I ask you a question? Oh, I'm sorry. Can I ask you two questions?

MARY. Sure.

DWIGHT. Why does Ty keep you locked up?

MARY. I ain't locked up.

DWIGHT. Oh.

MARY. What makes you think that?

DWIGHT. I don't know, I just figured –

MARY. You figured wrong. I could get out of here if I wanted to.

DWIGHT. Okay.

MARY. I like it down here. People leave me the hell alone. I got time to think, time to do my reading, my thinking. Don't have to answer no fool questions.

DWIGHT. I'm sorry, I –

MARY. It's where I live.

DWIGHT. Fair enough. Ain't never seen anybody live in a hole before.

MARY. Well you seen it now.

DWIGHT. Can you see down there?

MARY. I see all right. I can see you.

DWIGHT. How long's he plan on keeping you down there?

MARY. I told ya, he ain't keeping me anywhere.

DWIGHT. Then why don't you get out?

MARY. Maybe cause I don't want to. Why should I get out for you anyhow?

DWIGHT. Suit yourself.

(DWIGHT *turns to go.*)

Can I get you anything?

MARY. No.

DWIGHT. Good night.

(He stops to notice the stars peeking out over the horizon.)

Ooop…Big Dipper.

MARY. What's that?

DWIGHT. Big Dipper.

MARY. Where?

DWIGHT. Right in front of you. Maybe you can see it, straight ahead?

MARY. That ain't the Big Dipper, that's Orion. Dipper's behind you. Toward me.

DWIGHT. What?

MARY. Face me. That's the Big Dipper.

DWIGHT. Oh. Oh I see.

MARY. Sometimes people do that. They see Orion's belt and think it looks like the Big Dipper. People do the same thing with the Little Dipper. They think it's Pleiades. See, turn the other way, you see Orion, you see the belt?

DWIGHT. Um…

MARY. The three bright stars in a row, that's the belt. That's how you find him. And he's got his bow and arrow and then if you look in the winter, you'll see Scorpius, that's the Scorpion that killed him. And he's up there with his two dogs, still hunting.

DWIGHT. Wait, how do you know that?

MARY. I've seen the sky at night before ya dummy.

DWIGHT. No, but how do you see behind you?

MARY. There's a small window in the back. I can see out. Squat down, you can see right through. See it?

*(**DWIGHT** squats down so he's looking from front to back.)*

DWIGHT. Oh yeah. There it is.

MARY. You see it low to the ground like that, it looks like somebody taking a drink off the top of them mountains.

DWIGHT. How about that.

MARY. I got Orion in one window and the Little Dipper in the other. The beginning and the end, but nothing in between.

DWIGHT. You see the sun rise and the sun set, but you don't ever see it high in the sky. Is that it?

MARY. Yeah, kinda.

DWIGHT. The middle ain't worth much anyhow. That's where all the work gets done, right?

MARY. I don't know. Be nice to see the sun high in the sky sometimes.

DWIGHT. You ain't missing much. Come midday, it's hotter than a whorehouse on nickel night.

MARY. I wouldn't mind it.

DWIGHT. Thought you liked it down there?

MARY. Just when I start thinking you're okay, you gotta go put a spoke in the wheel.

DWIGHT. I just wanna know why he locks you up like you're some kind of…

MARY. What?

DWIGHT. I don't know. Carrot or something.

MARY. I ain't no carrot.

DWIGHT. I'm sorry –

MARY. You take that back.

DWIGHT. I said I'm sorry. Jeez. Never seen nothing like it.

MARY. Well, you have now.

DWIGHT. You cold down there?

MARY. No.

> (pause)

Come closer.

DWIGHT. Why?

MARY. I want you to see me.

> (**DWIGHT** *moves to the front of the cage, but hesitates.*)

Come on closer, vegetables don't bite.

> (**DWIGHT** *moves to the cage, knees down and peeks in.*)

DWIGHT. Where are you?

MARY. Here. You gotta put your head up to the gate.

> (**DWIGHT** *grabs hold of the gate and puts his face through the bars.*)

DWIGHT. *(pause)* What happened to your legs?

MARY. Nothing. They were always this way.

DWIGHT. Can you walk?

MARY. What do you think? Now you're looking at me all funny.

DWIGHT. Sorry, it's just…how come your head's that shape?

MARY. Cause when I was born, my Mama loved me so much, she squeezed me too hard and it stayed that way.

DWIGHT. Really?

MARY. That's what my Pa told me.

DWIGHT. You believe that?

MARY. No.

> *(pause)*
> You think I'm pretty?

DWIGHT. Sure. I guess.

MARY. No, I ain't.

DWIGHT. You're okay.

MARY. Tell me about Queenie.

DWIGHT. What about her?

MARY. How did you get her, was she given to you…

DWIGHT. No, she was a barter. I was an apprentice for a Smith, just learning the trade so I wasn't making much. And I did some work for a guy on the side, but then I found out he couldn't pay. So we dickered around a bit and he said, tell you what, I'll give you this mare. And I thought I got the good end of the deal, turns out she was crowbait. At least she was till yesterday.

MARY. You got a saddle on her.

DWIGHT. That I did.

MARY. You shoulda tried my idea.

DWIGHT. Aw, that'd never work.

MARY. How do you know? You gotta earn the respect of the animal. Didn't I tell you that? She's trying to see if you have what it takes to tame her.

DWIGHT. Come on…

MARY. How's she gonna respect you if she ain't seen you run with her yet? You try it. You tie that rope on, let her run, and hold on for dear life. If she finally tires out and you're still with her, she'll come back and be tamed. You'll see. She'll look at you like you deserve to ride her.

DWIGHT. It don't matter no more anyhow. She don't make a fuss at all.

MARY. You mighta ruined her.

DWIGHT. How do you figure?

MARY. You scare the daylights outta that horse she might just fold up and stop running altogether. Then she ain't no use to you either.

DWIGHT. I did what your brother told me to do.

MARY. Who said you had to listen to him?

DWIGHT. Aw, what the Sam hell do you know, you can't even walk.

(pause)

I'm sorry, I didn't mean that.

MARY. You should go home.

DWIGHT. I'm sorry.

(pause)

Why did Ty put you down there?

MARY. He says to protect me.

DWIGHT. From what?

MARY. He didn't see fit to leave me alone, is all.

DWIGHT. I never seen anybody locked up on account of trying to protect them.

MARY. Well, you seen it now, so why don't you just get on outta here and forget it?

DWIGHT. It must be tough.

MARY. What.

DWIGHT. Being left alone like that.

MARY. Like anything else, I guess.

DWIGHT. What do you do all day?

MARY. Read. Sing to my self a little.

DWIGHT. Really? I'd love to hear you sing.

MARY. Nah.

DWIGHT. Oh come on. Let me hear you.

MARY. Don't know you well enough.

DWIGHT. Well, what do you read?

MARY. Nothing you'd understand. Look, can you do me a favor?

DWIGHT. Sure.

MARY. There's a short pan on the porch there, next to the barrel. Can you fill it up with some well water for me?

DWIGHT. Okay.

(**DWIGHT** *moves to the porch to retrieve the water.*)

MARY. Ty was supposed to bring me some bacon, but I don't think I'm getting any tonight.

DWIGHT. Sure is a sound sleeper.

MARY. He'd beat the devil around a stump to keep from cooking. And once he's been on a bender, you might not see him for a day or so.

DWIGHT. How do you feed yourself?

MARY. I get by.

(**DWIGHT** *has the pan of water near the front of the cage.*)

Just set it down there. I need to wash.

DWIGHT. Okay.

MARY. You got a girl?

DWIGHT. No.

MARY. How come?

DWIGHT. I don't know. I had a girl. Sorta. But I don't see her much any more.

MARY. What happened?

DWIGHT. It ended.

MARY. That happens. Who was she?

DWIGHT. Can you keep a secret?

MARY. Sure.

DWIGHT. *(pause)* She was married to the guy I was working for.

MARY. Shoot. Does he know?

DWIGHT. Course not. And don't you go telling nobody neither.

MARY. Well, what'd you go telling me for?

DWIGHT. I don't know. Just don't tell nobody.

MARY. Who am I gonna tell? I never see nobody.

DWIGHT. Guess you're right.

MARY. Don't worry. My lips are sealed.

DWIGHT. Okay.

> *(pause)*

You know, I don't know if I could take it in a hole like that. I would start to get the shivers.

MARY. How come?

DWIGHT. I don't know. All dark and tight spaces like that.

MARY. It ain't so bad. You oughta join me some time.

DWIGHT. No way, I couldn't. Be too much like…

MARY. Like what?

DWIGHT. Being buried. I guess. When I was little and I found out that when you died they buried you, I remember I cried and cried. Went to my mama, "Mama don't bury me. I don't want to go down in the ground." Course, I wasn't thinking that you had to be dead first.

MARY. Not always.

DWIGHT. *(laughs nervously)* What are you talking about?

MARY. You ever heard of a dead ringer?

DWIGHT. No.

MARY. In England, the graveyards are real small and crowded. They run out of room sometimes so they would dig up coffins and use em over again. But when they dumped out the bones and looked inside, they found scratch marks on the lid of the coffin. Like people had been buried alive and were clawing to get out. So they started tying the wrist of the corpse to a string and they would lead the string out through the coffin to a bell in the graveyard. And if the person was buried alive, they could save themselves by ringing the bell. Hence the term, Dead Ringer.

DWIGHT. You're making that up.

MARY. It's true. Sure as I'm sitting here.

DWIGHT. I don't believe it.

MARY. Don't worry, nobody's gonna put you in your grave before your time. And even if they did, you'd get used to it.

DWIGHT. I would not. Hell no. I could never do like you, spending all that time alone.

MARY. Believe me, you get used to the solitude. After a while it becomes preferable

DWIGHT. *(shakes his head)* I like having people around. I don't know what I'd do if I didn't have somebody to talk to.

MARY. You go in to town a lot?

DWIGHT. Of course.

MARY. You see people you know.

DWIGHT. Yeah.

MARY. You drink with em, play cards, talk about this and that, and how are things out your way, and this one is marrying that one, and that one doesn't like this one and how is the weather, and I heard so and so might be passing through and this one died and isn't that too bad and that one had a little girl and isn't that just dandy. And then you go home by yourself and just before you go to bed at night you lie awake and wonder who the hell are those people? Do I know any of those people? Do they know me? Did I show them myself? Or did I just them the face that I want them to see? You think you're with all sorts of people, all day long, all sorts of faces, but they're just like you. All alone. Each and everyone of us. Cause nobody's in your world but you.

DWIGHT. But I can be with people if I want to. What can you do?

MARY. I got lotsa company. I got my two best friends, the wind and the stars.

(pause)

You go on home.

DWIGHT. You need anything else?

MARY. No.

DWIGHT. Okay. Good night.

MARY. Thanks for the water.

DWIGHT. Sure.

(He exits.)

MARY. *(quietly and to herself)* All the company in the world.

(blackout)

Scene Three

(Just past sunrise, the next day. **DWIGHT** *quietly makes his way toward the porch. He carries a small basket covered with a cloth. He looks around for movement and then slips over to the root cellar, kneeling ten feet from the entrance.)*

DWIGHT. **MARY.**. Mary, it's me, Dwight. *(pause)* Mary?

MARY. Good morning.

DWIGHT. Shoot. You scared me.

MARY. How come?

DWIGHT. I didn't think you were awake.

MARY. I been awake since sun up. What are you doing here?

DWIGHT. I brought you something.

MARY. What?

DWIGHT. You like biscuits?

MARY. I suppose.

DWIGHT. I made you some.

MARY. You did.

DWIGHT. That's right.

(He begins unwrapping the basket.)

MARY. You made me biscuits.

DWIGHT. That's what I said. Don't you think I can cook?

MARY. We'll see I guess.

DWIGHT. I can take em back if you don't want em.

MARY. No, I'll give em a try. Ty never made me no biscuits before.

DWIGHT. I wrapped em up so they stayed warm.

(He hands two biscuits on a napkin to **MARY** *through the bar.)*

They still feel warm to you?

MARY. Pretty much.

DWIGHT. What do think?

MARY. I'm chewing.

DWIGHT. Okay. They any good?

(pause)

MARY. I'm still working on it.

DWIGHT. You don't like em.

MARY. Dwight, these are hard enough to stop bullets.

DWIGHT. I just made em.

MARY. What's the recipe call for, sawdust and pigshit?

DWIGHT. I followed the same recipe my mother used to make. How come you don't like em?

MARY. Have you tried eating one?

DWIGHT. No. I was saving em for you.

MARY. Well, why don't you bite down on one of em.

DWIGHT. All right.

(He begins chewing one.)

MARY. A little tough, huh?

DWIGHT. I don't know, tastes pretty good to me.

MARY. Proves one thing. Your mother couldn't cook either!

DWIGHT. Aw come on now –

MARY. I'm sorry –

DWIGHT. I got up damn near two hours ago to make you biscuits –

MARY. I know –

DWIGHT. And all you can do is insult my mother –

MARY. I'm sorry. I appreciate the effort.

DWIGHT. Just trying to be nice.

MARY. Thank you.

DWIGHT. You don't even appreciate it.

MARY. I do.

(pause)

In the unlikely event that I get into a firefight with some Apaches, I'll be well prepared.

DWIGHT. How's that?

MARY. I can wrap my head in these biscuits and them arrows'll bounce right off.

DWIGHT. Is this the thanks I get for bringing you breakfast?

MARY. I'm sorry. Hey, sit down.

DWIGHT. What?

MARY. Sit.

> (**DWIGHT** *sits outside the gate.* **MARY** *begins singing. Her voice is clear and simple.*)

"Are you tired of me my darling

Did you mean those words you said

That would make me yours forever

On the day that we were wed"

> (**TYRUS** *appears on the porch, looking haggard and hungover.*)

DWIGHT. That's pretty. How's the rest of it go?

TY. Hey!

DWIGHT. Oh, hello Mr. Cole.

TY. Why you back so soon?

DWIGHT. Uh, well I was gonna give you the gun and the bullets. Remember? I only used but three and I wanted to get the change back from the ones I didn't use. And get my hat back.

> (**DWIGHT** *shifts uncomfortably as* **TY** *makes his way down the steps. He carries tin bowl of oatmeal.*)

I have em right here. He uh, she worked real good. I mean, the technique worked really good on Queenie. You shoulda seen her.

TY. All this goddamn singing so early in the morning, how the hell's a fella supposed to get any sleep?

> (**TY** *notices the biscuits and the napkin in front of the cage.*)

And what's this?

DWIGHT. Oh. I just thought that –

MARY. He brought em for me.

DWIGHT. Yeah, I got to thinking – to talking with Mary here –

MARY. Try one, they're real good.

TY. When were you talking to Mary?

DWIGHT. I came by last night, but you were asleep. To give you back gun and get the change for –

TY. And you made her some biscuits.

DWIGHT. Well, she said that she was hungry and you hadn't had time to feed her yet. So I just thought I'd make her some breakfast cause I knew I'd be back here today –

TY. I got your breakfast right here.

MARY. About time.

TY. Shut up.

(**TY** *kicks the cage. He puts down the oatmeal and picks up the remains of the biscuits. He holds them up in front of* **DWIGHT.**)

You ain't got no business coming back here to feed Mary, you understand?

DWIGHT. Yes sir.

TY. Take your biscuits and get on outta here.

(*He grabs holds up the remains of the biscuits and goes to crumble them and throw them at* **DWIGHT**'s *feet, but realizes they almost too hard to break.*)

Whoa. What'd you put in these, horsemeat?

DWIGHT. Why?

TY. I can't even crumble em with my hand.

MARY. Try chewing em.

DWIGHT. Aw, I was just trying to do y'all a favor.

TY. I feed her myself, you understand?

MARY. Shoot, I'd damn near starve to death waiting for you to make me something.

TY. *(to* **MARY***)* Oh yeah? How would you like it if I poured that good oatmeal out on the ground? How would you like that?

MARY. Go right ahead!

TY. Then you can just go hungry today, how about that?

DWIGHT. Oh, no, Mr. Cole –

TY. You shut up. You had no business being here.

DWIGHT. I know.

MARY. If you didn't drink so goddamned much, you wouldn't sleep half the night –

TY. *(overlapping)* Oh, pipe down –

MARY. – and maybe you'd get a meal on the table when you're supposed to.

TY. *(overlapping)* I got better things to do to be taking care of you –

MARY. Then why don't you just open this cage you put me in –

TY. *(overlapping)* Shut up!

MARY. You shut up. You the one who put me down here!

TY. *(overlapping.)* I'll fix you. I'll fix you good.

MARY. And then you don't take care of me or give me water or feed me or nothing.

TY. You want your breakfast?

MARY. Yeah, it's damn near lunchtime.

TY. Here's your goddamned breakfast.

(He picks up the oatmeal and dumps it through the bars. **MARY** *screams.)*

DWIGHT. Come on now –

TY. Eat it up. It's good. I worked all morning to make you your godammned oatmeal, I wanna see you eat it.

MARY. Leave me alone.

TY. Eat it!

(He kicks the cage again.)

Eat it up I said.

(Pause. **TY** *stands there glaring at* **DWIGHT**. *He shakes his head in disgust. After a moment, he disappears into the house.)*

DWIGHT. This is my fault, I'm sorry.

(He moves to the bars, picks up the napkin and starts to wipe the bars.)

I'm sorry.

MARY. Stop saying I'm sorry.

(He keeps wiping the bars.)

Leave it.

DWIGHT. No, I –

MARY. Would you just leave it?

*(***DWIGHT*** drops the napkin and looks around not knowing what to do. He then moves to the porch. Takes the three bullets out of his pocket, and lays them on the porch with the gun. He begins to walk away, but before he can leave, ***TY*** comes out the front door holding ***DWIGHT****'s hat.)*

TY. Hey. Forgot your hat.

*(***DWIGHT*** moves back to the porch. ***TY*** tosses the hat down to him.)*

DWIGHT. Thank you.

TY. What's your horse's name again?

DWIGHT. Queenie.

TY. How come you didn't ride her over here?

DWIGHT. Oh, I didn't ride her yet. But she's behaving herself real good. I got a saddle on her and everything.

*(***TY*** leans down and picks up the gun and examines the shells.)*

TY. You used three?

DWIGHT. That's right. But I did it just like you said. Worked like a charm.

TY. Glad to hear it.

*(***TY*** looks over at the cage and then motions for ***DWIGHT*** to follow him to the far end of the porch, ***DWIGHT*** follows. The two speak quietly.)*

She ain't right in the head.

DWIGHT. Who?

TY. Who. The Queen of England.

DWIGHT. Oh, you mean Mary. Yeah, I kinda figured that.

TY. She's all kinda trouble, you understand? It's all I can do to keep things going around here, make enough to feed the two of us, and she can't fend for herself at all. That's why I put here there, you see? Once, I left her alone and she damned near burned the whole house down. She ain't right.

DWIGHT. What happened to her?

TY. She was born that way. I shouldn't say this but my father wanted to put her down when she was little. He was ready to do it too. Just like one of his colts born with a bum foot, some such thing. She mighta been better off, hell if I know. My mother begged him to leave her be. Got so she didn't want to leave her alone with him for fear of what would happen.

DWIGHT. You can't kill somebody just cause they're a little different.

TY. No?

DWIGHT. No. I don't think so.

TY. *(pause)* You work with the Smith, that right?

DWIGHT. Yes sir. Mr. Wales. But I ain't worked for him going on four weeks now. Things has been slow.

TY. How you get by?

DWIGHT. Odd jobs, here and there. I had some of my father's money saved up too.

TY. I could use somebody around here to help clean up, take care of Mary. I'm driving myself crazy running back and forth to look after her. You be interested?

DWIGHT. Sure.

TY. I might need you now and then help out with some horses.

DWIGHT. Oh, I could do that. I can shoe em too.

TY. *(nods)* You got some time today?

DWIGHT. I wasn't going nowhere.

TY. I need you to ride with me to Donnelly's. He's got a buncha sick horses.

DWIGHT. Okay.

TY. Then maybe you can ride back and check on things, see if Mary got into any trouble.

DWIGHT. What kinda trouble could she –

TY. Look, you gotta get back here and keep and eye on her when I tell you, you understand?

DWIGHT. Yes Sir.

TY. If you're gonna work for me you can't be questioning me all the time.

DWIGHT. I understand.

TY. Good. Now, get saddled up. I'll meet you out front.

DWIGHT. Okay.

(**TY** *goes back into the house, but lingers in the doorway.* **DWIGHT** *then moves over to the cage.*)

Hey Mary? Looks like I'm gonna be seeing more of you. Your brother asked me to come on by and look in on you now and then.

MARY. Lucky me.

TY. Hey. Get saddled up.

DWIGHT. Yessir.

(**DWIGHT** *exits.* **TY** *watches him go. He reaches into the house, grabs his holster, shuts the door and moves down to leave. He stops at the cage for a minute.*)

TY. I'll send him back later on to feed you.

MARY. I'll be here.

(**TY** *exits. We see her two hands grip the bars firmly and give them a sudden shake. She then lets go and the hands disappear.*)

(blackout)

Scene Four

(Late Afternoon. Offstage, we hear TY *singing at the top of his lungs. He is quite drunk and muddy.* DWIGHT *walks alongside him. He too has been drinking but is relatively sober.)*

TY. *(singing)* "Are you tired of me my darling?
      Are you tired of me to-day?"

DWIGHT. I don't think –

TY. "Are you tired of me my darling?
      Are you tired of…"

DWIGHT. That's not it.

TY. What?

DWIGHT. That's not how it goes. The song.

TY. I know that.

MARY. Look who decided to come back.

TY. I was just testing you.
      "Are you tired of me my darlin…"

MARY. I'm tired of you.

DWIGHT. *(laughs).* Hey Mary.

TY. Nobody asked you.

MARY. Where the hell have you been? I'm starving here!

TY. I been working.

MARY. You been drinking.

TY. Working and drinking, drinking and more drinking.

DWIGHT. I'll fix you something Mary.

TY. You'll do no such thing. I will fix her supper. Just as
      soon as I take a rest.

*(*TY *plops himself on top of the root cellar with his legs
straddling the cage.)*

MARY. Dwight, would you mind going inside and frying me
      up some bacon?

DWIGHT. Yes, ma'am.

TY. Never mind. That's my job.

MARY. Well, if it's your job, why don't you go on and do it.

TY. Cause I'm resting!

DWIGHT. Mr. Cole, why don't you –

TY. Oh you call me Ty. You go right ahead.

DWIGHT. All right. Ty, why don't you just rest and –

TY. You know, you did a hell of a job today son. You were a lot of help.

DWIGHT. Thank you. Would you like me to go ahead and fix Mary some supper?

TY. No, I want you to sit here and have a smoke with me.

DWIGHT. I don't smoke, sir.

TY. Why the hell not?

DWIGHT. I don't know.

TY. Well, it's about time you started.

(He reaches into his pocket and pulls out two cigars.)

Sit down with me. Me, you, and Mary gonna have a smoke.

MARY. I'd rather have something to eat.

TY. Well, you're gonna smoke.

(He kicks the cage with his heel.)

You decide damn near everything else that happens around here, when to eat, when to shit, when to piss, when to clean up the shit and the piss. When do I get to decide anything?

MARY. You get to call all the shots.

TY. Like hell I do! Now me and this boy here are gonna smoke. And then we're gonna fix you some grub and there's not a damn thing you can do to stop us. What do you think of that?

DWIGHT. I'd be perfectly happy –

TY. Siddown!

*(He pulls **DWIGHT** alongside the root cellar, he hands **DWIGHT** a cigar and lights a match.)*

Take one of these. There's one for me.

(He lights his cigar.)

TY. *(cont.)* And there's one for you.

(He lights **DWIGHT** *'s cigar.)*

And one for **MARY.**

(He tosses the lit match down the root cellar, laughing.)

DWIGHT. Hey.

MARY. Ow.

DWIGHT. You stop that.

MARY. You bastard. Get off there.

TY. You're my beast of burden, you know that?

MARY. Get outta here!

TY. You done went and ruined everything.

(He lights another match.)

DWIGHT. Come on now, put that down.

TY. Shh. Watch this. Mary, you know what they used to call me in town? You know what?

MARY. No, I don't.

TY. Hot stuff!

(He tosses the match down into the cellar again.)

MARY. Sonovabitch.

DWIGHT. All right, that's enough now.

TY. What are you gonna do? Huh? Little Boy?

*(***TY*** *rises up and gives* **DWIGHT** *a shove.)*

DWIGHT. Let's just calm down now.

TY. You gonna calm me down Dew-ey?

DWIGHT. There's no need –

TY. Dew-ey! Mr. Dew-ey!

DWIGHT. You shouldn't be doing that!

TY. I'll do whatever I goddamn well please. You understand sonny?

(He grabs **DWIGHT** *by the collar.)*

TY. *(cont.)* You don't like it, you can just get your ass back home. Understand?

*(**DWIGHT** says nothing. But just stares at **TY**.)*

I'm going to catch some shut eye. You wanna spend all night talking to Mary Cock of the Walk, you go right ahead.

*(to **MARY**)*

That all right, sweetheart? I done found you a date, how's that? Huh?

(He kicks sand into the cage.)

I'm talking to you! And you ain't talking back, you beast.

*(**TY** moves up and onto the porch.)*

All right Mr. Dewey. That's your last chore of the night. Make the Virgin Mary in the hole some grub and if you would, please keep her company. Cause she gets so damned lonely sitting there night after night. She don't ever take into consideration for one minute what she's done to me! Never! Not for one minute.

(He moves into the house and can be heard still ranting and raving.)

Sick of it. You understand me? Sick of it!

*(After a moment, **DWIGHT** moves onto the porch. He retrieves the short pan and fills it with some water. He brings it to **MARY** and lays it outside the cage without a word. After a moment, **MARY** slides the pan into the cellar.)*

DWIGHT. Can I fry you up some bacon?

MARY. No. Thank you.

DWIGHT. You sure?

MARY. Not hungry.

DWIGHT. I got an apple. Ty brought it for the mares, but we never got around to feeding em.

MARY. What was wrong with them?

DWIGHT. Not eating. Couldn't pass nothing. All his horses were in a terrible way. Stomping the ground, kicking their sides. Ty thought it was sand colic so we spent most of the day walking em in circles. There's one stud colt that got settled down a little bit, but the other two was bucking something fierce. Donelly might lose em before this is through.

MARY. You gotta be careful when they get that way. One of em might twist a gut and roll right over you.

DWIGHT. Yeah.

(He reaches into his saddle bag and pulls out an apple.)

You sure you don't want none of this?

(After a moment, we see **MARY***'s hand emerge from the cage.* **DWIGHT** *hands her the apple.)*

You're welcome.

MARY. Thank you.

(pause)

How's your pink mare?

DWIGHT. Queenie? Good I suppose. I ain't seen her all day.

MARY. Strawberry Roan. I bet she got four white feet.

DWIGHT. That's right. Pretty as can be.

MARY. Shoot. A white hoof is soft, everybody knows that.

DWIGHT. Aw, that's a buncha whooey.

MARY. You got yourself a pink horse with four soft hooves.

DWIGHT. One of these days, I'm gonna ride her over here bare back and I'll have her jumping right over this root cellar, how bout that?

MARY. She sleeps lying down, don't she.

DWIGHT. All right, now how did you know that?

MARY. She's a dreamer. A horse that sleeps standing up can't dream.

DWIGHT. How come?

MARY. Cause the mare knows you need to be close to the ground to dream. You need to feel the earth turn one full rotation underneath you. Makes you know you're alive and that a day has passed. And when you know that it makes room in your head for the dreams to come. Animals know that, but a lot of horses are scared of their dreams. So they sleep standing up.

DWIGHT. "To sleep, perchance to dream, ay there's the rub."

MARY. Shakespeare.

DWIGHT. Yeah.

MARY. You can read?

DWIGHT. No, my father. He would read to us sometimes when were little. He had one of those big booming voices, you could listen to him say just about anything.

MARY. What happened to him?

DWIGHT. He passed on last June. So I got the land pretty much to myself. I might have to sell it though. He owed a lot of money on it.

MARY. Uh-huh. You know Blake?

DWIGHT. Who?

MARY. William Blake. He was a great poet. A real dreamer, he was.

DWIGHT. Like Queenie.

MARY. *(laughs)* Like Queenie. Yeah. He believed in spirits. Believed in them so much he thought they spoke to him more than the people he knew. Blake would look at trees and rocks for the whole day. He said he could look at a root, or a knot on a branch till it came alive and scared the daylights out of him.

DWIGHT. Sounds like a crazy man.

MARY. When Blake was young, he was an apprentice to an engraver. He kept having visions of his boss hanging from the gallows. Finally, he up and quit, couldn't take the image anymore. Ten years later, the boss was hanged to death for forgery.

DWIGHT. No kidding.

MARY. He wasn't crazy. He was a visionary. He saw things for what they truly were. Like you. Who do you think you are?

DWIGHT. What do you mean?

MARY. Well who are you?

DWIGHT. I'm...Dwight Foley.

MARY. I know that. But what are you? Are you your body? Your thoughts? Your soul? What makes you, you?

DWIGHT. I don't know, I never thought about it.

MARY. Did you ever think that maybe you are what you think of yourself? Like, if you imagine yourself to be something, that's what you'll become?

DWIGHT. Like what?

MARY. Anything. Or even if somebody else does it for you. For instance, I'll look at you and I'll imagine you to be something.

DWIGHT. Okay.

MARY. I imagine you to be St. George slaying the dragon.

DWIGHT. Oh, come on.

MARY. Sure, why not. I imagine you to be the avenger of my soul. I imagine you to be a lover, with a love so deep, all terrible and full of fury.

(*pause*)

DWIGHT. Okay, then what?

MARY. Then, it's all up to the imagination. We'll see if it happens. Blake believed that the imagination was the self. That we create the world in which we live.

DWIGHT. Do you think that's true?

MARY. It's true if you believe it to be true. If you don't think it's true, then you end up just accepting everything that comes your way.

(*pause*)

"Why was I born with a different face?
Why was I not born like the rest of my race?
When I look, each one starts! When I speak, I offend;
Then I'm silent & passive & lose every friend."

DWIGHT. How's the rest of it go?

MARY. I forget. Can I ask you two questions?

DWIGHT. *(laughs).* Sure.

MARY. Why'd you cheat with that girl?

DWIGHT. I don't know.

MARY. That wasn't right. She was somebody else's happiness.

DWIGHT. She was kind of a California widow. He never paid her no mind.

MARY. Did you love her?

DWIGHT. I found myself thinking about her all the time, got so I couldn't do much of anything else. So I guess I did.

MARY. Nah. You mighta just gone crazy for a spell. She pretty?

DWIGHT. I thought so. She had blonde hair and hazel eyes. Kinda plain when you first looked at her but then she'd smile and the whole world would light up.

MARY. What was her name?

DWIGHT. Darci. I was working for the Smith and he used to have me running errands. Always sending me up to the house, to get this and that, lunch or something. And her and me, we'd get to talking. Sometimes, she'd be waiting for me with a cold drink of water or lemonade. She was always so pleasant, happy to see me. And it got to where I would be working and thinking about nothing but finding excuses to go to that house, just to get a smile or a word, or a glimpse of her walking by. Got so if I got it, I could work, happy as could be. But then if I didn't get it, all I could think about was seeing her, doing something to get her to notice me, trying to figure out if she thought about me as much. And then one day, it was real hot, somebody paid with some greens and I had to bring em back to the house. And I rode up and brought that big basket up on the porch. And she must have been working in the yard cause I could see the sweat stains on her dress. And I just stood

there, looking at her skin glistening in the sunshine.
And real slow, she walked over to me, and she took
the corner of her apron and wiped my brow. Nearly
thought I was gonna faint. Then she put her mouth on
top of mine, and kissed me all hard and slow. And she
turned around walked into the house and left the door
open behind her. I followed her inside and took her
right then and there. Right in that kitchen. Only thing
that saw us was a basket full of snap peas.

MARY. Was she beautiful?

DWIGHT. She was the most beautiful thing I ever saw.
I remember putting my head on her chest with her
hand on my head. I tasted her, all wet and salty. I could
have died then and there.

MARY. Do you still see her?

DWIGHT. No. It was only that one time.

MARY. No, do you still see her. Naked. In your dreams.

DWIGHT. All the time. Every night.

MARY. How come you're not with her?

DWIGHT. Next time I saw her, she made like nothing had
ever happened. Just one of those things I guess.

MARY. Maybe she got scared.

DWIGHT. Maybe. Anyway. I don't go visiting the house
much anymore.

MARY. Everything ends.

DWIGHT. Yeah.

   (pause)

You know what? I don't like the way Ty treats you.

MARY. Neither do I.

DWIGHT. No. I don't like it one bit.

MARY. He won't have me around much longer.

DWIGHT. What do you mean?

MARY. He's gonna have me sent away. I heard him talking
to a guy from Lubbock who runs a home, place where
they send crazy people. Ty's saving up his money and
once he's got enough, he's gonna have me put away.

DWIGHT. He wouldn't do that.

MARY. The hell he wouldn't. I heard him say. He don't know I heard it, but I know it's true.

DWIGHT. That's terrible.

MARY. Yep. Well, maybe I'll just come live with you then. How about that?

DWIGHT. Aw, I couldn't take care of you.

MARY. Sure you could. You could feed me and I'd read you poetry at night till you fell asleep.

DWIGHT. Yeah? And what are we gonna live on?

MARY. I know where Ty keeps his money.

DWIGHT. Sure. The First National Bank.

MARY. No. There's 500 dollars right under your feet.

DWIGHT. Where?

MARY. Don't play dumb. Hell, everybody in town knows about my daddy and his big jar of money.

DWIGHT. I don't.

MARY. When my Pa walked out on us, he took half the money he had and he left the other half behind. About the only the good thing he ever done. He put it in a big glass jar and gave it to Ty. Now I seen where Ty buried it. He adds to it about once a month. Gotta be at least five bills in there. You play your cards right, you can have half of it.

DWIGHT. How's that?

MARY. One of these days, you're gonna do me and the whole world a big favor and get rid of him.

DWIGHT. What do you mean?

MARY. I mean one day, you will kill Tyrus Cole.

DWIGHT. Now, wait a minute.

MARY. You just said you didn't like it one bit.

DWIGHT. But that don't mean –

MARY. You wanna see me put in a home?

DWIGHT. No, but –

MARY. Then you're going to help me. See, I'm just like William Blake. Didn't I tell you that? Blake could see everything that was alive in everything that was dead. I can see what everybody's gonna do before they do it.

(**MARY** *extends her pistol through the bars of the gate.*)

Take this.

DWIGHT. What's that for?

MARY. For you to kill Tyrus.

DWIGHT. I ain't killing nobody.

MARY. Yes, you will. Cause if you take care of him, half that money will be yours. More money than you ever seen in your life.

DWIGHT. What makes you so sure?

MARY. I know things. I live below the earth with everything that's constant. I watch the stars and I listen to the wind. I become the dirt you feel beneath your feet. See…

(*She reaches her hand out and uses both hands to lay the gun out on the ground in front of the bars.*)

…I knew you would come one day. Hell, I could feel you coming before you even decided to get that damn horse of yours fixed.

DWIGHT. Yeah?

MARY. You're drawn to me.

DWIGHT. Come on.

MARY. You find me hideous and enchanting all at the same time. Your feelings are all a jumble cause you just can't figure me out. I'm like the Smith's wife. You can't stop thinking about me. Only this time, you'll never stop. Cause you and me are part of the same dream.

DWIGHT. I never killed nobody.

MARY. No. Don't suppose you have. But one day, you will.

DWIGHT. How?

MARY. I'm gonna make you.

DWIGHT. If you know what's gonna happen, why don't you do it yourself?

MARY. And then what? Turn it on myself? Besides I never get a clean shot to him. Tyrus is very careful, he walks in front of me real quick, he ain't never given me a good shot. But you'll get a good chance, you mark my words.

DWIGHT. Do you think he knows you wanna....

MARY. I don't know. But put it this way, he ain't taking no chances, that's for sure.

(pause)

You think you came here to take care of Queenie? You came here to take me away from this place.

DWIGHT. I'd like to, but –

MARY. Come on. I don't wanna die in this hole.

DWIGHT. Let me think about it.

MARY. You're supposed to help me.

DWIGHT. I ain't never killed nobody.

MARY. You hate him just as much as I do.

(She thrusts the gun at him. **DWIGHT** *reaches for the gun. He cradles it in both hands.)*

DWIGHT. I can't.

MARY. Go in that house and take care of him.

DWIGHT. No.

MARY. Careful, it's loaded.

DWIGHT. I gotta think about it.

MARY. What's to think about?

DWIGHT. I can't just up and do that. I gotta think about it, all right? I ain't saying yes or no, I'm just saying....let me sleep on it, all right?

(He holds the gun out for **MARY** *to take back.)*

MARY. No, you hold onto it.

DWIGHT. I ain't even got a holster.

MARY. Aintcha got a saddle bag or something?

DWIGHT. Yeah, but –

MARY. Well just keep it in there till you need it.

DWIGHT. I'm going home.

MARY. Okay, you go sleep on it. But the more you sleep on it, the worse it's gonna get.

DWIGHT. What do you mean?

MARY. You ain't gonna be able to stop thinking about it. I'm gonna be all over your dreams like a Stud on a Chestnut Mare in the spring.

DWIGHT. Mary –

MARY. I'll let you have me all ruddy and sweet to eat.

DWIGHT. I wish I could help you –

MARY. You working with him tomorrow?

DWIGHT. I suppose.

MARY. Then tomorrow night you'll get another chance.

DWIGHT. I wish I could help you but –

MARY. Go home, go to bed, dream a little. And you watch, all night long, you'll be dreaming of the good stuff you can do with that money.

DWIGHT. That's what I'm worried about.

MARY. If it worries you then, why don't you try to sleep standing up?

DWIGHT. Good night.

MARY. Good night.

(*He exits.*)

Sweet dreams.

End of Act One

ACT TWO

(Morning. TY is downstage left, a ways away from MARY's cell, working with some rope and a saddle. After a moment DWIGHT enters holding a saddle bag. He stops, realizing that TY hasn't noticed him yet. He moves back, hand squarely on the bag.)

(TY continues to labor on the saddle. He rubs it with some soap, trying to work out a rough spot. DWIGHT lifts the top of the saddle bag to reveal the gun MARY gave him. He looks to MARY's cell for support. After a moment, TY looks up, startled. DWIGHT thrusts the gun back in the bag.)

DWIGHT. Good morning.

TY. *(overlapping)* Shoot. How long you been standing there?

DWIGHT. I just got here.

TY. You trying to scare the hell out of me?

DWIGHT. No.

TY. Jesus Christ.

DWIGHT. I was just –

TY. Hell, I didn't even hear you coming.

DWIGHT. I didn't want to disturb you.

TY. Trying to scare the hell out of me.

(Pause. TY goes back to working on the saddle.)

DWIGHT. Good morning.

TY. Morning.

DWIGHT. How's Mary today?

TY. Leave her be. She's sleeping.

DWIGHT. Oh.

TY. Take a hand here.

DWIGHT. Do you want some coffee?

TY. Had some.

DWIGHT. I could make more.

TY. That's all right. Hold it out straight.

*(***DWIGHT*** picks up the slack in the rope.)*

Damn thing never sits right. It's been bugging my leg something awful.

DWIGHT. Nice day today.

TY. Yeah.

(noticing the saddle bag)

What you got there?

DWIGHT. Huh? Oh, this is just a bag my father used to have. Figured I could use it.

TY. Let me see it.

DWIGHT. It ain't nothing.

TY. Looks like it's hardly been used.

DWIGHT. Yeah, my Pa didn't like it too much. It was always hanging up behind the door and I thought –

TY. Hand it over. I been looking for something like that.

DWIGHT. Ain't nothing in it. I brought Mary some more of my biscuits.

TY. Hell, she don't want none of them. Let me see that bag.

DWIGHT. Oh, uh –

*(He walks over to **MARY**'s cell.)*

I think she's up.

TY. She ain't up, she hardly slept a wink.

DWIGHT. Mary?

TY. Shh. Would you keep quiet?

DWIGHT. What's the matter with her?

TY. How the hell would I know?

DWIGHT. Mary, how you feeling this morning?

TY. Will you shut up? Leave her be.

DWIGHT. Should I make something for her?

TY. Like what?

DWIGHT. I don't know. Breakfast or something?

TY. You can feed her when we get back.

DWIGHT. That might not be till nightfall.

TY. Then I guess she'll have to wait till then.

DWIGHT. Let me just leave her something.

(**DWIGHT** *goes to the cell and kneels down by the gate.*)

TY. I said no.

DWIGHT. I made her these biscuits.

TY. They almost killed her the first time.

DWIGHT. I'm just gonna leave em.

TY. Goddamnit!

(*moves over to the gate, grabs the saddle bag and tosses it across the yard*)

What the hell is the matter with you?

(*The two men face one another.*)

DWIGHT. (*quietly*) Just trying to feed her, is all.

TY. I said no.

DWIGHT. All right.

(**TY** *stares at* **DWIGHT**, *examining him.*)

We gonna keep walking em today?

TY. Yeah.

DWIGHT. Those horses sure are sick.

TY. Well, they got gravel in the gut. What the hell's the matter with you? You're acting like a cat in heat.

DWIGHT. Oh, I don't know. Just anxious to get going. Hey I was wondering, what if they don't get better.

TY. Who? Donnelly's horses? They'll get better.

DWIGHT. What if they don't?

TY. You some kinda old lady? I just said they'd get better. And if they don't, we shoot em.

DWIGHT. For real?

TY. Well, we don't fix em up, we'll lose em anyway.

DWIGHT. You ever put a horse down before?

TY. Part of the job.

DWIGHT. I guess.

TY. It's the best thing. Can't watch an animal suffer like that. Ah, don't you worry. I got a few more tricks up my sleeve. Saddle up Bullet for me.

(**TY** *moves to the porch to close the house. After a moment,* **DWIGHT** *retrieves the saddle bag.*)

DWIGHT. Why do you suppose she couldn't sleep last night?

TY. I don't know. She gets headaches, can't sleep, can't hold anything down. She's all sortsa fucked up.

DWIGHT. Mary's a smart girl.

TY. Uh-huh.

DWIGHT. I kinda like her.

TY. Yeah? How come?

DWIGHT. She reads poetry. She sings like an angel.

TY. That don't amount to a hill a beans.

DWIGHT. I think she's kinda…beautiful. In her own way.

TY. Are you right in the head?

DWIGHT. You ever looked at her?

TY. I look at her every day.

DWIGHT. No, I mean, really looked at her?

TY. I don't know what you drank for breakfast Son, but I want some of it soon. Cause that girl is a mess.

DWIGHT. No, if you look at her long enough, something starts to happen. You get used to how her head is all, knotted kinda. And then the knots get all smooth and you begin to imagine what she might have looked like if….well, things had gone different.

TY. You mean if her Ma had lived?

DWIGHT. I don't understand.

TY. She got a fever after giving birth to Mary. Died a week later.

DWIGHT. I didn't know that.

TY. Now you do.

(Pause. TY begins to walk away again.)

DWIGHT. How come you keep her in a hole anyways?

TY. *(stops, turns, and stares at DWIGHT for a long moment)* Mary wants to be in the hole.

DWIGHT. Huh?

TY. She asked me to put her in there.

DWIGHT. What for?

TY. It's too early for these questions.

DWIGHT. She's suffering, poor girl.

TY. You think I don't know that? I don't like this any better than she does. I'm sicka the whole damn situation. If I had my way, I'd be miles from here.

DWIGHT. Then why don't you up and leave?

TY. I can't.

DWIGHT. Why not?

TY. Cause before my mother died, I promised her I would take care of Mary.

DWIGHT. Oh. That was big of you.

TY. That was stupid of me. I made a promise. What the hell for? Damned if I know, cause no one asked me to. I had to go and open my big mouth. Why? Cause I thought it was the noble thing to do? Some shit like that? Who knows, maybe my mother would have been happier if I left her to die right then and there. No mother can want a life like that for her daughter.

DWIGHT. Wasn't her fault she was born that way.

TY. Wasn't mine neither. It was somebody's mistake, but I'm the one who has to keep paying for it. Pa up and left and I been taking care of her, going on ten years now. Can't go nowhere, can't get married, nothing. Hey, I'm sorry for her all fucked up like that, but I have other places to go. Just cause she's in jail don't mean I have to be the jailer. You understand?

DWIGHT. Well, I think you should feel proud that you keep a promise –

TY. Lotsa people make promises. If no one else is keeping them, what does that make me? Some kind of a sucker, that's what. You go head and keep a promise. Let me see you find the guy who can do it. Son, you're either the fucker or the one's getting fucked. Sooner you find out, the happier you'll be.

DWIGHT. I'm sorry. I didn't mean to tell you your business.

(pause)

TY. Look, Mary don't want outta no hole. The hole was her idea in the first place Got so she was so ashamed of her appearance, she was so afraid of being left alone, she wanted in the hole. Now I can't get her out of the damn thing. Don't you think I would if I could?

DWIGHT. I guess. I just hate seeing her suffer that way.

TY. One of these days I'm aiming to do something about it.

DWIGHT. Like what?

TY. I don't know. Can't go on like this forever, that's for sure.

(pause. TY looks at DWIGHT for a long moment.)

I once had to put down a mare that was constricted. Name was Sally. Pretty horse, deep chestnut, big white streak across the muzzle went back around to the nape. She was in a bad way and there wasn't no getting out of it. Rearing up, kicking all about the place, horse was in a whole lot of pain. But every time I raised that gun up to the back of her head, she would stop, suck up the pain, stop kicking, hold it together. Like she was saying to me, see? I can take it. No matter what this life can dish out, I can take it. Cause it's all I know. My life is pain, and it's gonna be nothing but pain from here on out. But if that's what my life is gonna be, then so be it. Cause I don't know what's on the other side of this thing. And her eyes would get big and brown and there wasn't nothing I could do but lower that gun and leave her alone and let her roll and kick and rear up and we just would start the whole thing all over again.

(pause)

You ever shot anybody?

DWIGHT. No, sir.

(Pause. **TY** *looks at* **DWIGHT** *and then looks over at* **MARY***'s cell. They both look at* **MARY***'s cell for a long moment.* **DWIGHT** *stares straight ahead and speaks quietly.)*

TY. Hard to watch a loved one suffer.

DWIGHT. I know what you're thinking. And I ain't interested.

TY. No. I didn't expect you would be. I got a place I can send Mary. Not the nicest place in the world, but at least they can take care of her better than me.

DWIGHT. Oh?

TY. Yeah. Just waiting till I got enough saved for her upkeep.

DWIGHT. That's good.

*(***TY*** nods.)*

What every happened to Sally? The mare?

TY. She died. Died on her own. I sat there with her all night, watching her twist and turn, till she passed. I coulda killed her but I didn't. I ain't nothing but gutless.

(After a moment he walks back to the house.)

Let's get going.

*(***DWIGHT*** remains staring at* **MARY***'s cell.)*

(blackout)

Scene Two

(Noontime. **DWIGHT** *walks in holding the saddlebag. He climbs up on the porch and gets himself a drink of water.* **MARY** *calls to him from the cell.)*

MARY. Hey.

DWIGHT. Hey.

MARY. Where are you going?

DWIGHT. Getting a drink.

MARY. How's it going with the sand colic?

(pause)

Dewey!

DWIGHT. What?

MARY. I asked you a question.

DWIGHT. I heard you. It's going fine.

(He moves down and kneels down by the cell.)

Look, I ain't got much time. Ty said he'd make you some supper later on. But I got some of these biscuits, and there's a piece a pie there too from Donnely's wife. I thought it was pretty good.

(Pause. **MARY** *reaches out and takes the biscuits.)*

Ty said you had a pretty bad night. How are you feeling now?

MARY. Okay. Come closer.

DWIGHT. What?

MARY. Look inside here.

*(***DWIGHT*** *puts his face right up to the grate.)*

DWIGHT. That's very pretty. Where did you get that?

MARY. It was my Ma's.

DWIGHT. Oh that's nice.

MARY. It was her wedding dress.

DWIGHT. You must uh…you keep it in some kinda case down there?

MARY. I got a trunk back here, see? Got all sortsa things in it, old clothes, books and things.

DWIGHT. It's in very good condition. Looks very nice on you.

MARY. Really?

DWIGHT. Yeah, it does.

MARY. It's the first time I ever wore it. Doesn't feel like I thought it would. I thought it would feel more special somehow. But something's only new once, you know? After that it becomes part of your thoughts, part of everything you carry with you. You think it'll feel new tomorrow?

DWIGHT. Maybe. Sometimes when something's new it feels that way for a while. Some things always feel new. You never get settled into them.

MARY. That's why we fall in love so much. It always feels great when it's new. Once you settle into it, it's on its way to becoming something else.

DWIGHT. It could be settling into something better.

MARY. Probably not.

(pause)

I decided I was going to wear it on some special occasion. This seemed as good a day as any.

DWIGHT. Why's that?

MARY. Cause today's the day I get outta this hole.

DWIGHT. Oh.

MARY. "He loves to sit and hear me sing
Then laughing, sports and plays with me;
Then stretches out my golden wings,
And mocks my loss of liberty"

DWIGHT. Who's that?

MARY. Blake. *(pause)* You know, I haven't been outside this hole so long, I think I forgot what it was like.

DWIGHT. When was it?

MARY. Oh, a long time ago. Tyrus would take me into town with him now and then. If he had to do some work with a horse somewheres, or if he had to go into town for supplies. He'd strap me to the top of the wagon so I could sit up and he could leave me while he went and ran his errands. I remember one July, we rode in. It had rained for two days straight and the road was dark and full of mud. Tyrus was buying some feed and he musta stopped for a drink or two cause I was sitting there by myself, felt like forever. Propped up on top of that wagon like some kinda freak for the whole town to see. People would pass by, gawking at me, saying things, like, "Hey, how come your head is so big? Looks like some kinda melon gonna burst in the sunshine." Children would throw pebbles at me, trying to get my head to bust open. Their mothers would rush them away, "Oh I'm terribly sorry miss, he don't know no better, is there anything I can do for you?" "Well yes there is as a matter of fact. You can find me a new body to exist in cause this one has failed me pretty good. How's about I borrow yours for a week or two." And they'd rush off cussing under their breath.

(pause)

And then this one man, climbed right up next to me on the wagon. Sat right down and introduced himself as Mr. Laurence Alger III, all perfumed, wavy hair, strange looking fella. Bulgy brown eyes. He was a smooth talker, knew how to use his words. He said that he ran a traveling show with all sorts of strange and unusual acts. And would I like to join him? There was a sword swallower and a bearded lady and they even had a little boy with a tree growing out of his hand. And there was very good money in it and, he said, "My dear, you could turn this terrible misfortune into a great windfall for you and your family." And I started thinking, maybe he's right. Maybe I should live with some other people. Folks who were…kinda like me. And I figured right then and there, it was either join him and his circus, or get used to spending lots of time by myself. Cause I sure as hell wasn't coming in to this town again. I said to him, "No, thank you for the offer sir. And would you kindly get off my wagon, before my brother returns and gets any ideas?" Cause I knew Tyrus would have sent me off to the traveling freak show faster than you can set a prairie fire in August. That was the last time I went to town. And I'll never go back again. It's a town full of lying eyes and painted faces.

(pause)

DWIGHT. Shoot, I forgot to get you some water.

(He moves back to the barrel on the porch.)

MARY. Never mind that.

DWIGHT. No, no, I got it.

MARY. Get back here.

DWIGHT. What?

MARY. Come here.

*(**DWIGHT** moves back to the gate.)*

Look at me. When you and Ty come back here tonight, I'm going to ask him to come close to the cellar and look at my dress. When he leans down in front of the gate, you're gonna kill him.

DWIGHT. I can't.

MARY. And then you're gonna open this gate and you're gonna get me out of this hole. And you can have your way with me.

(pause)

And you can hold me and we'll look at the stars and I'll read you poetry. And then you'll feel my mouth all over you. I'll make you forget Darci and everyone you ever laid eyes on. Wouldn't you like that?

DWIGHT. Yes.

MARY. When I put on this dress this morning I was thinking of you.

DWIGHT. Why do we have to kill him?

MARY. Because he's gonna have me put away.

DWIGHT. Let me just open this up and get you outta there and we'll just find the money and leave.

MARY. Don't you think he'll come looking for us?

DWIGHT. Nah, he might be a little upset, but he just wants you out of his hair. Besides, we don't need the money.

MARY. The hell we don't. And that money is mine.

DWIGHT. Just tell me where it is, and I'll get it.

MARY. I can't. I have to get out to show you.

DWIGHT. Why?

MARY. It's complicated.

DWIGHT. I can't do it Mary.

MARY. Don't you want to help me?

DWIGHT. Yes.

MARY. You said you would.

DWIGHT. I didn't. I said I'd think about it. Jesus, you're talking about killing a man.

MARY. People die every day.

DWIGHT. Don't mean I gotta be the cause of it.

MARY. All right, get on outta here.

DWIGHT. Aw, come on now.

MARY. I don't wanna hear it. You're about as useful as tits on a bull, you know that? If you can stand to see me cooped up here, getting abused and tortured like he does, then what kind of a man does that make you?

DWIGHT. Mary. –

MARY. You tell me that. What kind of a man?

DWIGHT. Even if I did kill him, so what then? What are you gonna do then?

MARY. You get me outta this hole, we get the money, and then we lickety-split on out of here.

DWIGHT. Bullshit. Your brother says it was you who wanted in that hole in the first place.

MARY. What?

DWIGHT. He said you were embarrassed cause of the way you looked and you wanted to be shut up in there so no one could see you and now he can't get you out of it.

MARY. And you believe that?

DWIGHT. Hell, I don't know.

MARY. Don't you think I'd get outta here if I could? You think I like having that bastard rattle my cage and throw shit down at me whenever the hell he's on a bender? Would you like that?

DWIGHT. Well, what am I supposed to do about it?

MARY. You're all mouth, that's what you are. Everybody wants to tame the finest stallion but ain't nobody wanna get their boots dirty. "I don't like the way he treat you." Comes to doing something about it, you don't care a continental, do ya?

DWIGHT. I'm scared, all right?

MARY. You're scared? I'm the one looking at the rest of my life in a goddamned grave.

DWIGHT. I never even fired a gun before!

MARY. Bullshit, you fired one at that dumb horse of yours, didn't you?

DWIGHT. No, I didn't.

MARY. You said you did.

DWIGHT. I didn't. I lied. I tried to do it, I chickened out. I took one look at Queenie and she was rearing up and I pointed that gun at her and I just couldn't do it. I just kept a few bullets to make it look good.

MARY. Jesus Christ, if this don't shove the queer, I don't know what does.

DWIGHT. I'm sorry.

MARY. Yeah, me too.

DWIGHT. I wish I could help you. Cause I think it's the right thing to do and…you're a different kinda person. But…

(pause)

Shoot, I gotta be getting back.

MARY. Uh-huh.

DWIGHT. Anything else I can get for you?

MARY. Nope.

DWIGHT. You want some water or something?

MARY. Ain't thirsty.

DWIGHT. Okay. I come back it'll be nightfall. Maybe we can look at some stars or something.

(*pause*)

Did you see Orion last night? Man,that came up clear as could be.

MARY. I didn't see it.

DWIGHT. Orion the hunter. You'd swear he was alive.

MARY. He is alive. He's more alive than you.

DWIGHT. How's that?

MARY. What makes you alive and him dead? How long has he been up in the sky fighting that bull? Long before you've been here. And he'll be up there long after you're gone. Way I see it, he's more alive than any of us. He's sure as hell more alive than me. He's up there every night, his belt in the sky, bright as can be. I'm down here in the dark. Some people say they got one foot in the grave. Hell, I got that beat. I got my whole damn body down here just waiting for death to come.

DWIGHT. I gotta go.

MARY. Dwight, if you killed someone, you figure that's the worst thing you could ever do?

DWIGHT. Yeah, I suppose.

MARY. And the worst thing you've ever done up to now.... that would be…what?

DWIGHT. I don't know.

MARY. Maybe fucking somebody else's wife?

DWIGHT. Yeah.

MARY. The smith would be madder than an old wet hen if he found out about that now, wouldn't he?

(*pause*)

MARY. *(cont.)* In fact, I know if you're gonna be a philanderer, you'd better either have a lot of money, or a quick draw. And you ain't got either.

DWIGHT. What are you saying?

MARY. You'd better find some time today to get used to firing that gun. Cause when you and Ty come back tonight, you're gonna be firing it at him and you're gonna shoot him dead. And if you don't, I'm gonna tell Tyrus all about you and Little Darci, wife of the Smith. He don't know the Smith all that well, but he knows him well enough. And I know he'd be telling him first chance he gets. And when the Smith finds out, there's no telling what he might do.

DWIGHT. You wouldn't do that.

MARY. Wouldn't I? We can do this nice or we can do it dirty, but we're gonna get it done.

DWIGHT. I can't believe you'd do that.

MARY. You made a promise to me.

DWIGHT. I did no such thing.

MARY. And you're gonna keep it.

DWIGHT. I didn't promise you nothing.

MARY. I'm getting out of this hole Dewey. And you're gonna help me do it. Now you think about that on the way back to Donnelly's. Tyrus must be missing you by now.

DWIGHT. Mary, I can't –

MARY. Shut up. I'm through being patient with you, you flannel mouthed liar. You're nothing but half broken sentences. I'm stuck in this goddamned hole and I got more gumption than you.

DWIGHT. I never fired a gun.

MARY. You're gonna fire one now. Go on.

(Slowly, **DWIGHT** *picks up the saddle bag, and heads out.)*

Have a nice ride.

(blackout)

Scene Three

(There is a light change to indicate the passing of time. After a moment, we hear **MARY***, singing from the cell, the same song Tyrus sang in Act One.)*

Are you tired of me my darling
Did you mean those words you said
That would make me yours forever
On the day that we were wed

    Tell me could you live life over
    Would you make it otherwise
    Are you tired of me my darling
    Answer only with your eyes

Do you ever rue the springtime
When we first each other met
And spoke with warm affection
Words my heart will ne'er forget

    Tell me could you live life over
    Would you make it otherwise
    Are you tired of me my darling
    Answer only with your eyes

(possible cut, depending on costume change)

Do you think the bloom's departed
From the cheeks you thought so fair
Do you think I've grown cold hearted
'Neath the load of woman's care

    Tell me could you live life over
    Would you make it otherwise
    Are you tired of me my darling
    Answer only with your eyes

Scene Four

(DWIGHT runs in, bloody and out of breath. He paces back and forth, but he cannot seem to calm himself down.)

DWIGHT. My God, my God –

MARY. What is it?

DWIGHT. Sweet Jesus –

MARY. Dwight?

DWIGHT. Sweet Jesus, forgive me –

MARY. Dwight, what the hell are you –

DWIGHT. My God, My God.

MARY. All right willya calm down?

DWIGHT. I can't.

MARY. Just sit, for Chrissakes.

DWIGHT. No!

(He takes the saddle bag off his shoulder and hurls it at the front of the cage.)

MARY. Stop that!

DWIGHT. Jesus Christ.

MARY. Would you sit down?

DWIGHT. I can't. I need water.

MARY. All right get yourself some…

(He bolts up to the porch and douses himself with some well water.)

DWIGHT. What did I do?

MARY. …water. Go head.

DWIGHT. What the hell did I do?

MARY. Are you gonna tell me what happened?

DWIGHT. I wish I'd never met you. I wished I'd never seen the two of you godforsaken people in my entire life. All I wanted was to tame my horse, to get my ass on the mare that some sumbitch gave me in a bad deal, that fucking mare. Fucking Queenie, if I had never gotten that stupid horse I'd never woulda met you.

MARY. Dewey! What happened?

DWIGHT. Your brother's dead.

MARY. What?

DWIGHT. He's dead.

MARY. You did it.

DWIGHT. Well, no –

MARY. What do you mean, no? You did it, right?

DWIGHT. Sorta.

MARY. What is sorta? You can't be sorta dead. You're either dead or you ain't. Jesus Christ, you could screw up a free meal.

DWIGHT. Would you let me finish? Donnelly had gone into town and the two of us were there, working the stallions, walking em around, and they started getting better. Except for this one big horse…named Jeremiah. He was 20 hands, easy. He was a rare breed and he had a nasty disposition and the colic only made it worse. Well, Ty started walking him in circles, trying to loosen his gut, you know? Bust it out of him. But the horse wouldn't slow down. He kept running faster and faster, till he was all lathered up and then just like that, he stopped. Dead on a dime. And he turned real slow to where he was facing Tyrus, moving his front hoof up and down, pawing at the earth, like he was calling him to get closer. I told him, I said, "Ty, I don't like the look of this. You best be careful." Ty just shoved me aside and said, "Aw, don't worry about a thing. Old Jeremiah and me, we gonna be friends. Right Jerry?" And Ty pressed up to him, trying to rub his stomach. He brought his ear up real close, to the sides of the horse, when all of a sudden, Jeremiah reared up on two feet and rolled right onto the ground, with your brother underneath. Me and Donnelly, we tried to grab hold of him, but Jeremiah kept bucking and kicking like the devil. We couldn't get near him. The horse was rearing and rolling like he was trying crush bones into the dirt. And then Tyrus got to his knees and it looked like was gonna escape when Jeremiah gave a quick kick, hit him square on side of his head. And Ty fell like the life was knocked right out of him. And his mouth fell open and it was full of blood and sand and his face was all black except for the whites of his eyes. And he whispered to me, all scratchy like, "Help me, Dwight. Help me." And then he didn't say nothing no more.

(pause)

DWIGHT. *(cont.)* I couldn't move. I stood there looking at that horse with Tyrus in between us, lying lifeless in the dirt. And then the horse turned his head cock-eyed, kind of curious like. And he moved real slow till he was standing right on top of the body, and then he just pissed all over him. Like so much rain. Warm rain falling from a horse named Jeremiah. I turned around and I ran. I blew over that fence and jumped on Star and I rode him here as fast I could.

(pause)

I stood there and watched Mary. I stood there and I watched while your brother was killed. And I did nothing. I killed him. Just like you said I would.

MARY. *(quietly)* Anybody follow you here?

DWIGHT. I don't know. I don't think so.

(pause)

I killed your brother.

(DWIGHT *has calmed down and now takes on a more steely, reserved tone.)*

MARY. You didn't kill nobody.

DWIGHT. I did. I coulda stopped it.

MARY. You couldn't a stopped shit. My brother's a lot tougher than you and couldn't wrestle away from that stallion, what makes you think you coulda done anything? Just an accident that's all. Way he trained horses, he had it coming.

DWIGHT. How can you be so cold?

MARY. Runs in the family.

DWIGHT. My pa, used to say, "You walk with a cripple, you soon begin to limp." And you know what, he was right. Cause I'm starting to think just like you two.

MARY. You finally did something right.

DWIGHT. No. It wasn't right. And I hate you for that. Both of you. I'm a God fearing man. And I don't mean to curse the dead, but you got blood on my hands now. And I don't care if it was the right thing to do. It was the wrong thing for me.

MARY. It's a cold world Dwight. You just found out the hard way.

DWIGHT. Yeah.

    (*pause*)

You owe me some money.

MARY. For what?

DWIGHT. For killing your brother.

MARY. In good time.

DWIGHT. Give me the money.

MARY. You gonna open this gate for me?

DWIGHT. Where is it?

MARY. I can't show you from down here, now can I?

DWIGHT. Just tell me where it is.

    (*pause*)

Come on, where's the money?

    (**MARY** *begins to laugh.*)

What's so funny? What's so Goddamn funny?

    (**DWIGHT** *kicks the cage.*)

MARY. I know just what you're thinking?

DWIGHT. Oh yeah?

MARY. You're thinking about leaving me down here, ain't you?

DWIGHT. No.

MARY. Then why don't you open the gate?

DWIGHT. Look, I filled my part of the bargain. I did your killing for you –

MARY. You didn't fill part of nothing. You didn't kill anybody. Hell, it was just an accident and you were standing by. You think you made your balls on that? You was just lucky, that's all.

DWIGHT. Where's the goddamn money!?

MARY. Where the hell do you think it is?

DWIGHT. All right. You don't want to tell me? Fine. You ain't going no place. I'll torch the whole damn place if I have to, but I'll find that money.

MARY. You know, Ty was a mean sonovabitch and I hated him just as much as you. But he was right about a lot of things. He told me, deep down, all men are greedy bastards. They'll sell you up the river for a whole lotta nothing. "We are arrant knaves all, believe none of us."

DWIGHT. I ain't listening to you.

MARY. You wanna know what else he said?

(**DWIGHT** *continues to look about the porch.*)

It was actually something he told you. I wonder if you were smart enough to believe it.

DWIGHT. What?

MARY. Sure you wanna hear it?

DWIGHT. I'm listening. What, what?

MARY. It's a secret. You gotta come close.

(**DWIGHT** *hesitates.*)

Aw come on, I ain't gonna bite you. You got plenty of time to find that money. I sure as hell ain't going nowhere. And Ty ain't coming home to catch you looking. Come down close.

(**DWIGHT** *kneels in front of the cage.* **MARY**'s *hand reaches out suddenly as she grabs* **DWIGHT** *by the collar. Her voice takes on a different tone, a strong loud whisper, as if a snake has found its voice.*)

I love it in this hole. I don't EVER want to leave.

DWIGHT. What?

MARY. I said, I don't ever want to leave this hole. See, I crawled down here one day. And I got used to it. And now I can't imagine living anywhere else. Tell me that don't take the rag off the bush!

DWIGHT. You're crazy.

MARY. I remember, I was here alone one day and Ty left me in the yard with nothing but some water and a parasol or some such thing. And I was lying there in the heat, baking something fierce. Sun was hanging over me like some kinda vulture. So I just kinda slithered across the yard till I made it into the cold dark earth, just as if I was an old rattler or something and I ain't come out ever since. See, all that time, Ty was telling you the truth. I couldn't stand it up there in the bright, feeling it on my face and my back and my legs. All that light shining on me, reminding me of my own wretchedness. But in the darkness, everything's the same. Down here in the earth, the only thing that matters is what you think and what conjure and what you imagine. Whatever I create, that's what I am.

DWIGHT. Fine. You wanna live underneath the ground, you can stay there!

MARY. Don't matter. I won't have to do it much longer.

DWIGHT. How you figure?

MARY. I'm dying. Tyrus knew how sick I was. He used to see me cough up blood every morning. He knew I didn't have long. That's why I wanted him dead. I couldn't stand him living up there without me. Made me sick to my stomach. Everybody's gotta die, but I couldn't stand the idea of him living in this world after I left it behind. If I gotta go, I'm going to bust the place up on my way out.

DWIGHT. Okay. You're gonna tell me where that money is, I'm going to take the half you owe me and I'm going to get the hell out of here. And never come back.

MARY. I told you, I don't owe you nothing.

DWIGHT. You owe me what you promised!

MARY. You didn't *do* what you promised!

DWIGHT. All right, suit yourself. I'll just turn this place upside down till I find it.

MARY. Till you find it? Where do you think it is?

DWIGHT. I bet it's in that house somewhere.

MARY. Nope. I told you. Tyrus buried it.

(**DWIGHT** ignores and her and heads to the house.)

Now, if you were him, where would you put it? No sense digging up a hole, when there's already one dug. And what would be really good is if you put the money where somebody could keep an eye on it.

(pause)

The money's down here with me. It's been down here all along. See, it's in a jar sitting right on my lap. Like I was nursing some little baby girl. Been here all this time. And if you want it, you gotta come get it.

DWIGHT. Give it to me.

MARY. How bad you want it? Kick open this cell, come on down here, and see if you're man enough to take it from me. What's the matter Dewey? You scared? Scared to come down in my dark hole and get what you want? It's real cool down here. Pretty deep too. Good six feet, some parts eight feet, maybe more. Who knows? Maybe this root cellar is endless. Maybe you come down here and you'll never come out.

(In a rage, **DWIGHT** grabs the gun from the saddle bag. He fires a shot at the lock holding the gate shut. He rips it from his hinges and stands back.)

DWIGHT. Hand it to me.

MARY. No.

DWIGHT. Give me the money!

MARY. Come get it.

(**DWIGHT** cocks the gun at her.)

DWIGHT. Don't make me shoot.

MARY. You want the money, don't you?

DWIGHT. You bitch.

> (**DWIGHT** *fires a single shot into the hole. He then fires another and another. With each shot, we hear* **MARY** *groan, and then she is silent.*)

> (*He stands there for a long moment, catching his breath. He hesitates and then places the gun at the front of the root cellar and dives in. We hear him moving about the hole and then after a moment,* **DWIGHT** *emerges, covered with mud, and holding a glass jar. It's black and covered with dirt. He laughs as he puts the jar down, spilling the contents. Bills are spread out over the ground. The bills are old and dirty, but there's quite a few of them in small bundles.* **DWIGHT** *begins to collect them furiously.*)

> (*Suddenly,* **DWIGHT** *writhes in pain. He starts a couple of times and then falls in a heap, into the money and the mud. As he falls, we see* **MARY**'s *hand holding a bloody dagger. Her arm is covered in white lace which is stained with blood and dirt. She drops the knife to the side and brings her hand down hard, grabbing* **DWIGHT**'s *back.*)

MARY. See Dwight? In time, everyone returns to the earth. Life's nothing but a lot of running around in the light....

> (*We never see* **MARY**'s *face only the single arm dragging* **DWIGHT** *down toward her.*)

...searching for a tunnel into the darkness.

> (*Slowly, his body is dragged down into the hole. It should have the effect of a snake, slithering back into the earth.*)

Time for sleep now. Let's you and me have a nice long rest.

> (*We hear her sing softly as the lights fade to black.*)

Are you tired of me my darling?

Did you mean those words you said

That would make me yours forever

On the day that we were wed...

Blackout – End of Play

OTHER TITLES AVAILABLE FROM SAMUEL FRENCH

APOSTASY

Gino DiIorio

Drama / 1m, 2f

Sheila Gold, 55, a successful Jewish businesswoman suffering from terminal cancer, is spending the end of her life in a comfortable hospice where her only companion is her 30 year old daughter, Rachel. The two have a tense relationship as Rachel has spent most of her adult life working at Planned Parenthood and is generally a disappointment to her entrepreneurial mother.

While in the hospice Sheila has become fascinated by a late night televangelist, Dr. Julian Strong, a black man in his 50's. She finds his message inspiring and comforting and she writes Strong, offering to make a sizable donation to his ministry. Much to her surprise, Strong flies out to visit Sheila, presumably to see her sign the check in person. His physical presence is even greater than his TV persona and the two fall head over heels in love. Sheila begins to toy with the idea of converting to Christianity and spending her final days with Strong's church in California. This revelation upsets her daughter to no end as Rachel is certain that Strong is a crook, promising hope and salvation, when all he really wants is to come between her and her inheritance.

Is Strong truly in love with Sheila or is he only out for her money? Sheila must choose between her daughter and a new love and life-style, in what will certainly be her final days.

"Playwright Gino Dilorio has done an amazing job of presenting religion with a nice blend of faith and cynicism. This production is full of outstanding performances, surprise twists, and will keep you riveted from start to its amazing finish."
– *Upstage Magazine*

OTHER TITLES AVAILABLE FROM SAMUEL FRENCH

PALESTINE, NEW MEXICO

Richard Montoya

Drama / 7m, 6f

Rumors, Secrets, Sand and Blood. U.S. Army Captain Catherine Siler journeys to the New Mexico reservation home of Private First Class Raymond Birdsong on a search for answers. The questionable circumstances surrounding Ray's death in Afghanistan create a crisis of conscience for the captain giving her no choice but to re-examine her own life along the way.

Richard Montoya and Culture Clash, L.A.'s premiere Chicano performance group, return with a play about America's constantly shifting political landscape exploring loss, identity and the notion of occupied homelands. Palestine, New Mexico promises to be an inherently theatrical work that mixes humor and cold fact to unforgettable and galvanizing effect.

"... Lunatic Irreverence... a rich premise and another sign of Culture Clash's ambition to plumb new multicultural depths of meaning by broadening its Chicano worldview."
– Charles McNulty, *Los Angeles Times*

"Outrageous imagery and serious subtext ... a gallery of pungent and often moving character portraits..."
– Bob Verini, *Variety*

"Richard Montoya [is] up to some of [his] old tricks... mixing satire, farce, plain silliness, pathos and tragedy..."
– Jay Reiner, *The Hollywood Reporter*

OTHER TITLES AVAILABLE FROM SAMUEL FRENCH

DREAMLANDIA

Octavio Solis

Dramatic Comedy / 6m, 3f

Inspired by *Life is a Dream*, the towering achievement of Spanish drama, Dreamlandia explores the terrain between illusion and reality. Set in the borderlands between Mexico and Texas, this haunting new play vibrates with the clash of cultures, NAFTA, narcotics, and illegal immigration. In an everchanging world, family, cultural and sexual identities collide.

"In Teatro Vista's provocative staging of Solis's latest work, Márquez meets Beckett in a surreal, tragicomic telenovela. Here the U.S.-Mexico border isn't so much a patrolled place as a state of mind."
– *Time Out Chicago*